# THE
# WELL
# HOUSE

*Inspired by True Events*

# ERNEST SOLAR

INDIEOWL
PRESS

INDIEOWL
PRESS

4700 Millenia Blvd
Ste 175 #90776
Orlando, FL 32839

info@indieowlpress.com
IndieOwlPress.com

# THE WELL HOUSE

Cover Design & Interior Layout by NightOwlFreelance.com
Cover Photograph © Ira V. Gustin

Manufactured in the United States of America

Paperback ISBN-13: 978-1-949193-87-9

For all the boys and girls whose voices are never heard.

"Something lives only as long as the last person who remembers it." ~A very old Indian saying

# THE
# WELL
# HOUSE

# Part I

# PRESENT

"Taa daaa!"

"Wait, play that again," said Farah, still wearing the headphones.

Gannon used the touchpad mouse on his laptop to slide the tracker on the editing software to play the recording again. This time he pressed the loop button and then the triangle play button. The two-second recording played repeatedly in a loop cycle. He watched the reaction on his fiancées face.

Farah cupped both hands over the headphones to block out any extraneous noise. Eyes closed, she listened to the recording repeat itself. "Taa daaa! Taa daaa! Taa daaa! Taa daaa! Taa daaa!" She pulled off the headphones and handed them back to Gannon. "She's saying 'Taa daaa!' in a singy song voice. It's a little girl. Almost like when Payton does a cartwheel and finishes with a 'Taa daaa!'"

Gannon smiled at her. "This was recorded at 2 a.m. in the

1

middle of the forest away from any of the walking trails."

Farah shrugged her shoulders and moved off toward the kitchen. "She is saying 'Taa daaa!'"

Gannon closed his laptop. He moved into the kitchen to help Farah with dinner. Shuffling the chicken around in the frying pan Farah asked, "Wasn't the recorder near that old farmhouse?"

Gannon nodded his head. "Yeah, it was up the hill from the old Griffith house."

Farah thought for a moment. "Maybe a little girl used to live there? Maybe she was a slave?"

Gannon pulled the plates out of the cupboard for dinner. He wouldn't say that Farah was a psychic or medium. However, she did have a sixth sense about things. She just seemed to *know* things. Since moving into their house a year ago, she had several dreams-if you want to call them dreams, more like visitations from the old woman, Julie, who used to own the house. At first, they weren't sure if it was Julie, but at the community potluck dinners a couple of the neighbors described Julie. They talked about her mannerisms, the way she dressed, her routine, and Farah and Gannon were able to deduct that who visited Farah at night was Julie. Farah never got the sense that Julie was malicious. But seeing a ghost can be unnerving in its own right.

Gannon had his own experiences; however, they were different. He usually heard movement. Or sensed a presence. Many times, while working from home, he caught himself checking the closets because he swore a physical person was secretly hiding in their house. Never finding anyone, his next logical conclusion was that he was hearing Julie move around the house. Gannon was a trained scientist. Therefore, he errored on the side of skepticism. Gannon would be the first to admit that he had to control himself from automatically jumping to a paranormal explanation. He forced himself to eliminate all other logical possibilities before believing or accepting that a ghost was living in their house.

The one exception was Farah. Gannon wasn't sure if Farah knew or not; he suspected she knew, but she was his barometer. If Farah suspected paranormal activity, Gannon was one-hundred-percent onboard. He still tried to eliminate all logical possibilities. But in the back of his mind he was doing a happy dance when Farah believed something originated from the paranormal.

"So, you're saying I picked up the voice of a ghost?" asked Gannon.

"A spirit," corrected Farah.

Gannon chuckled. "I go out there trying to capture the howl of a Bigfoot and come away with the voice of a spirit."

Farah smiled. "Oh, Bigfoot is out there. He was just laying low that night."

Gannon smiled. "I'm sure our neighbors think we're nuts."

Farah dished out the chicken and rice onto the plates. "Oh, I'm sure." She replaced the skillet on the stove. "That recording also had the cannon boom, right?"

Gannon nodded his head. "Yeah, about an hour later."

Farah mixed her chicken and rice together. "If that was a real explosion or cannon we would have heard it and we would have awoke."

# Part II

# IN THE PAST

L ucy ran from the front porch of the house as fast as she could toward the small creek that ran across the front yard of her parents' house. When she reached the edge of the creek, she pushed off with her right foot and leapt as far as she could across the creek. She felt her body sail through the air and cross the creek in one long jump. Her left foot came down with a loud splat as it struck the swampy ground on the other side of the water. Muddy water splattered her bare legs, summer dress, and sandals as Lucy continued to hop and skip away from the swampy area that peppered the ground from the creek to the barn. When she reached the solid ground of the dirt driveway that led up to the main road, she stopped and examined her muddy shins. She quickly tried to rub the dirt away before shrugging off the thought that her mother would be cross with her.

Lucy wondered what to do for the day. She had already gathered the eggs, milked the cow, and helped her mother in the kitchen making apple pie for dinner. School was out of session for an undetermined amount of time because Miss Emily was sick. She knew her mother would want her to practice her arithmetic and writing, since it technically was a school day. Lucy hoped reading the Bible after dinner tonight to the family would count as practice and she wouldn't have to do extra reading before bed. Lucy glanced at the family barn and saw the farmhand, Harvey, inside the structure tossing hay bales from the loft into the stalls. She watched him for a moment as he worked. She liked Harvey. He was cute with strong muscles and sandy brown hair. Whenever she thought about him she got a tickle in her belly. She told her mother once about the tickle and her Ma laughed at her. Not in a mocking or hurtful laugh. A silly laugh that girls share with each other when they tell secrets. Her Ma hugged her tight and said, "You've always been boy crazy." Lucy wasn't sure what that meant. She thought boys were fun and cute. Her Ma walked away from the conversation with a smile and shake of her head saying, "I fear that day you are 16 Lucy." Sixteen was only six years away and Lucy didn't understand what that meant.

Lucy called out, "Hi, Harvey!"

Harvey looked up from the loft of the barn and waved to Lucy. "Good morning, Lucy! Your' hair looks lovely in the morning light."

Lucy felt her cheeks turn hot and the smile on her face stretch even further. Absentmindedly, she raked her hand through her long golden blonde hair. Wanting to keep his attention, Lucy called out, "Watch this, Harvey!"

Knowing that he was watching her, she took two quick steps forward and then propelled herself onto her hands and then her feet again as she performed a flawless cartwheel. When she landed on her feet again she raised her arms high and said, "Taa daaa!"

Harvey dropped his pitchfork, wildly clapped his hands, and whistled. "Way to go, Lucy!"

Lucy blushed and smiled at Harvey's response. It was the same every day. Harvey never failed her on being happy to see her, giving her a warm smile, or cheering for her cartwheels - even if he had seen over a thousand of them. She waved to him and called back, "I'm off to see if Luke is home."

"Have fun," said Harvey as he picked up the pitchfork to get back to work.

Lucy turned and ran up the hill that lead to Luke's house. Luke was the boy who lived next door to their farm. Luke was a couple years older than her, but they went to school together. He was cute, but not as cute as Harvey. She liked Luke. Luke made her laugh and was always willing to play games with her. She figured he would be home. She just hoped that his father would let him play for the day.

The trail to Luke's house ran through the small patch of forest along the creek that passed through both of their family farms. Lucy either skipped along the large stones in the creek or along the edge. When she reached the property line of the two farms, she carefully squeezed herself through the barbwire fence. Lucy knew the purpose of the barbwire was to keep the cattle from both families separated, even if they were branded. She picked her away through the trees toward the small pond. Stepping beyond the tree line, she froze. Joe-Michael was by the Well House next to the pond. Joe-Michael was the farmhand that helped Luke's father. She didn't like Joe-Michael. He was a tall man with a thin frame. He didn't have muscles on his arms like Harvey. Joe-Michael's dark hair was stringy and oily. His clothes were always dirty, and he smelled like a mixture of pigs and skunks.

Lucy stood for a moment watching Joe-Michael before deciding what she was going to do. She could slip back into the tree line and follow the trees to the driveway that led to the main road. From the main road she could walk down to Luke's house, but that would add another thirty minutes. Or she could continue on her way past the pond up to Luke's house that was sitting atop the small hill in front of her. Lucy took a deep breath to gather her courage and calmly, but quickly, started to walk along the edge of the pond. Lucy hoped that she was small enough to be able to slip past Joe-Michael without him noticing.

Lucy reached the midway point of the pond before Joe-Michael turned around and saw her. She forced herself to keep walking. He called out, "Miss!" Lucy turned her head toward him, smiled, and waved. Joe-Michael neither smiled nor waved. He just watched her walk by and up to the house. *Creepy*, thought Lucy.

# Part III

# PRESENT

Farah and Gannon skipped across the creek in the fading light of the setting sun on their daily walk. They passed the abandoned barn that the deer used as shelter during rainstorms and moved up the steep hill. As they walked the air felt different and darkness descended faster than normal. At the top of the hill, the sky was a mixture of reds, oranges, and purples in the west, and the moon was shrouded in white mist to the east. Without saying a word, they both stopped and looked around at the trees and sky. Gannon asked, "Where are we?" Which was a silly question because they both knew they were walking on the trails in their neighborhood. Farah hesitated before answering, "Somewhere different."

Gannon understood what she meant without asking her to explain. Something was different. They were somewhere different. Often at night Gannon and Farah would play cards, drink wine, and talk for hours about the mysteries of life. One subject they usually visited during their nightly conversations was the existence of alternate dimensions. They believed these alternate dimensions paralleled and intersected with their own dimension. They believed it was possible for animals and some humans, to slip through dimensions via portals. The portals could be found where the veil from two connecting dimensions is thin. Gannon and Farah both believed their home and community were at the intersection of a thin veil that separated several alternate dimensions. Often, they felt as if they had slipped in and out of alternate dimensions without their knowing. Therefore, Gannon was not surprised when Farah confirmed his thoughts that the hill upon which they stood may look like the one they could see from their kitchen window, but in many ways was a completely different hill all together.

"You hear that?" asked Farah.

Before Gannon answered, he heard the laugh of a little girl, followed by the laugh of a man. "I think so." At times Gannon was reluctant to confirm when he heard something because he didn't always trust his own hearing due to his family history of poor hearing.

"Sounds like a lil' girl and a father laughing," said Farah.

Gannon nodded his head in agreement and looked around the field of grass that blanketed the hill. He expected to see their neighbor, James, and his daughter, Emily, crest the hill.

"Sounds like they are coming this way," confirmed Farah.

Again, Gannon nodded his head. Farah reached out and clasped his hand, tugging him along the trail. As they walked they continued to hear the girl and what they assumed to be her father, laughing. When they reached a fork in the trail they heard a cow moo behind them. Gannon and Farah glanced behind them to confirm there was no cow. They took the path to the right and commented at how the night sky and stars looked different. The air smelled different to them. The energy in the field felt electrified. They descended the hill along the path, expecting to see the little girl and her father on the trail that looped around the base of the hill. As they reached the bottom of the hill and turned in the direction toward their house, however, the sky flickered, the air shifted, and the wind blew. Gannon and Farah stopped and looked at each other. "I guess we're back," commented Farah with no enthusiasm in her voice.

Gannon nodded his head in agreement. They must have stepped through the veil back into their own reality because the sky, the smells, and the energy felt familiar. Gannon commented, "I don't hear the girl anymore."

Farah listened. "Maybe it was the little girl in your recording?"

"Hmm, maybe," said Gannon.

They clasped hands and finished their walk home in content silence.

# Part IV

# IN THE PAST

L ucy ran to the barn from the front porch of the house to find her dad. He stood by the open gate with an angry look on his face. Lucy asked, "What's wrong, Pa?"

Her father glanced at Lucy's face and flashed her a big smile. She felt his anger melt away with his smile. He shook his head and said, "Harvey left the gate open again and Bella is on a jaunt."

Bella was the family's cow. Bella provided the cream for the milk and butter that the family used. Lucy knew that her father wasn't that upset because Bella wouldn't have gotten far. She was probably over the hill chewing on some fresh grass. Lucy reached out and grabbed her dad's hand and said, "I'll help you find her." Her father smiled and said, "Sounds like a treat for me." Lucy hugged her father's strong arm as they turned to walk up the dirt driveway to the top of the hill. She always felt safe and protected when her father was around.

As Lucy and her father climbed the small hill they talked

and laughed about everything. Her father asked questions about school and her friends. She would tell him stories of what she experienced throughout the day and he would give a laugh that resonated with the wind. Lucy would giggle in return, feeling like she brought pure joy to her father. Sometimes he would chase her through the grass, which only made her laugh even harder. Or he would grab her around the waist, throw her over his shoulder, and spin her until they were both dizzy.

They heard Bella moo on the opposite side of the hill and without a word changed direction. They crested the hill and saw Bella being led by Joe-Michael. Involuntarily, Lucy squeezed her father's hand. He looked down at her with a quizzical look on his face. Lucy felt momentarily embarrassed that her father recognized that something was wrong. However, her father had always been able to read her like one of his favorite books. She leaned into her father's arm and looked up at him as she came to a stop. He lowered his ear closer to her and she whispered, "He scares me."

Her father looked at her and then Joe-Michael. He stood up straight, squeezed her hand for reassurance, and moved toward Bella and Joe-Michael. When Joe-Michael was about ten yards away from Lucy and her father, he nodded his head and said, "Sir."

"Thank you, Joe-Michael. I apologize for the trouble," said her father.

Joe-Michael shook his head. "No trouble, Sir. I was clearing some trees by the pond and saw ole' Bella here wanderin' by the fence. I know if it was my cow wanderin' I would want someone to bring her back too."

Lucy's father reached out and took the rope from Joe-Michael, tugging on it to get Bella's attention. She lifted her head from a fresh patch of grass and mooed once in annoyance. He tugged again, and she began her slow walk up the hill. Lucy turned to follow Bella; glancing over her shoulder, she saw her father shake Joe-Michael's hand and nod. He then turned and walked away. Joe-Michael turned back toward the other farm and disappeared among the trees.

Lucy, her father, and Bella walked in silence until they reached the top of the hill. As they started to descend the hill, Lucy realized that during their walk the sun had set behind the mountains in the West. She squeezed her father's hand and smiled at him as she gazed up toward him. He returned the smile and said, "Never judge a man by his appearance. Just his actions." Lucy knew her father was referring to Joe-Michael. She glanced over her shoulder and then nodded her head that she understood, even though she really didn't.

The next morning was a Saturday. Lucy woke early to attend to her chores before running off to her friend's house to play for the day. From the front porch of the house, she saw her father speaking with Harvey by the barn. Her father made hand and arm gestures pointing toward Bella and the hill. She hopped down the front steps and skipped through the yard to the creek. She leapt from rock to rock to cross the creek to the barn. Her father had finished the conversation with Harvey and was walking toward her. When he saw her he smiled, nodded his head, and said, "Good morning, Lucy."

Lucy smiled and replied, "Good morning, Pa."

Lucy could tell that the smile on his face was forced. She watched him for a moment as he walked back up to the house. She then turned her attention to Harvey and smiled. She waved at him and said, "Good morning, Harvey!"

Harvey glanced at her and mumbled a good morning.

She climbed on the fence to be as tall as Harvey. She leaned against the railing and asked, "What's wrong?" He used the pitchfork to move hay around the feed pen. Without looking at her, Harvey said, "Aw, your Pa's cross at me for letting Bella out last night."

Lucy snickered and said, "But Harvey you've done that before."

Harvey shot her a look that made her blood turn cold. Then, just as quickly, the look on his face vanished and he smiled. He shook his head and turned his attention back to the hay. "I forget is all."

Lucy nodded her head in agreement. She forgot things from time to time also. She hopped off the fence to go start her chores.

Harvey called out, "Hey, Lucy—I got you something." She turned around and saw Harvey leaning on the pitchfork, smiling at her.

"You did?" asked Lucy with more than a hint of excitement in her voice.

Harvey laughed. "Yes, I did," he replied with an exaggerated southern drawl. He motioned for her, "Come I'll show you."

Lucy quickly opened the gate, slipped in, closed the gate, and chased after Harvey.

Harvey slowed his pace for her to join him.

They walked into the barn and Harvey dramatically waved his arms in front of him in the direction of a red bicycle with white-wall tires leaning against one of the horse stalls and loudly proclaimed, "Taa daaa!"

Lucy stared at the bicycle in shock. She slowly walked toward it, worried that if she got too close it would disappear, like a dream. When she reached the bicycle, she touched the handlebars. It felt real to her. She spun on her heels and threw herself into Harvey's stomach and chest. She gave him a tight hug and kept saying over and over again, "Thank you, thank you, thank you!" Harvey hugged her back. When she released the hug and attempted to push back, it took a moment for Harvey to let go. She turned back toward the bicycle and pulled it from the wall. "Why?" she asked, turning to look at Harvey.

"A beautiful girl deserves a beautiful bike," said Harvey with a sly smile.

Lucy felt her cheeks get hot. She looked away from his smile. She jumped on the bicycle and rode it out of the barn into the feed area. She kicked open the gate and sped out to the dirt driveway.

Harvey chased after her.

Lucy peddled as hard as she could, going up the hill until her legs could no longer propel the bicycle forward. She hopped off laughing and panting for breath.

Harvey raced up behind her carrying a camera and shouted, "Let me get a picture of you with the bike!"

Lucy proudly stood behind her new bicycle on the hill and stretched her smile from ear to ear.

Harvey snapped the picture.

At the bottom of the hill, Lucy saw Bella meandering through the open gate from the barn. She called out to Harvey, "Oh no, Bella is getting loose again!"

Harvey muttered "Damn," loud enough for Lucy to hear. He spun on his heels, racing back down the hill to catch Bella before she strayed too far.

Lucy smiled as she watched his lean body race down the hill. Holding the handlebars to her bicycle, she pushed it the rest of the way up the hill toward Luke's house. She knew he would be ridiculously excited to see her new bike.

# Part V

# PRESENT

Gannon opened his eyes and saw Farah staring at him. She smiled, reached out and touched his face and said, "I just love your face." Gannon smiled, closed his eyes and pressed his forehead against hers in embarrassment. He whispered, "You can't watch me while I sleep."

Farah laughed. "But it's one of my most favorite things to do."

Gannon kissed her and then rolled on to his back to stretch. He moaned loudly as he stretched his arms over his head and twisted his body to work out the stiffness in his muscles. Farah giggled and scooted over next to him when he was finished to press her body against his. She asked, "Did you sleep well?"

Gannon nodded yes and then remembered a dream he had. "I think I had a dream about that lil' girl last night. You know the one that said, 'ta da'?"

"Was it scary?"

"No, it was brief. I saw her standing on the hill holding a

13

red bike with a proud smile on her face, as if she was getting her picture taken." He paused and thought about it more. "She was proud of it."

"Maybe it was a present," said Farah.

"Yeah, I think so."

Farah asked, "What are you going to do today?"

Gannon smiled at her. "I should cut some of the grass in the neighborhood. I've been slack on doing my share this summer."

"I'll help," said Farah.

Gannon smiled, "I'll get the mower and bring it down to the house, and then we can clean up some of the walking trails on this side of the neighborhood."

Farah smiled and kissed him. She rolled out of bed and moved into the kitchen to start breakfast. As she moved down the hallway, she woke the house up with her soft voice as she sang.

Gannon dressed in old jeans, a long-sleeve shirt, and a bandanna on his head to ward off poison ivy and ticks. Gannon and Farah ate a hearty breakfast of eggs, sausage, and potatoes before starting their weekend chores. Farah cleaned up the dishes as Gannon walked the trail to the red barn to retrieve the riding lawnmower. As he descended the path from his yard he turned left toward the pond. Through the trees he spied a young man walking along the far side of the pond near the Well House of the spring. Gannon peered at the young man wondering who he was. He had only lived in the neighborhood for a little over a year and knew that he had not met all of the neighbors yet. Gannon figured the young man was one of the elusive neighbors or maybe a family friend visiting for the weekend. As he moved closer to the Well House he noticed that the young man had sandy brown hair and wore dirty overalls. The clothes reminded Gannon of something an old-time farmhand from the early 1900's would wear. He smiled to himself because it wouldn't surprise him if the young man was wearing something from that time-period.

As he got closer to the Well House Gannon called out to the young man, "Good morning," and lifted his hand to wave.

The young man turned and looked at him with a glint of malice. Gannon narrowed his eyes in response. Something didn't feel right about the situation. He clenched his fists in his work gloves and felt as if a confrontation was going to ensue. Gannon would never consider himself a fighter, but he wouldn't shy away from a fight either. The young man spun on his heels and rounded the corner of the Well House away from Gannon. Gannon paused for a brief half-step and then continued on his way with a wide arch around the Well House. He watched the Well House to make sure the young man wouldn't come around the corner and try to attack him. As Gannon rounded the Well House the young man was gone. He paused for a moment and looked around, suspecting that he would see the young man fleeing through the brush and trees. But he didn't see or hear any movement. Gannon slowly circled the entire Well House and couldn't find the young man. He peered into the small structure and knew the man would never fit in the Well House. "What the hell?" muttered Gannon to himself.

Farah was out front using the push lawnmower to cut their own yard.

Their neighbor, Bryan, was out front pruning his trees.

Gannon pulled up and cut the engine to the mower and called out, "Bryan!"

Bryan looked up from his trees and smiled. He waved and walked over to Gannon. He nodded his head toward the riding mower, "Doing some cutting?"

Gannon smiled. "Yeah, I figured the West Side needed a bit of trimming on the trails and stuff. You know, trying to do my part."

Bryan nodded his head in agreement.

Gannon asked, "Hey who's the young guy with sandy brown hair that lives in the neighborhood?"

Bryan gave Gannon a quizzical look and tilted his head to the side. "I don't know."

"Hmmm, maybe he's not a neighbor then," said Gannon.

Bryan asked, "Where did you see him?"

Gannon nodded toward the pond, "Down by the pond this morning. Young guy, muscular build, sandy brown hair, wearing overalls."

Bryan turned toward the pond and pointed to the house near the pond that was barely visible through the trees. "You've met Rich, right?"

Gannon nodded. "Yeah, it wasn't him."

Bryan shook his head. "Maybe he was visiting Rich?"

Gannon shrugged. "Probably. I was just curious. Seemed like something was off about the guy. His look rubbed me the wrong way."

Bryan smiled. "Have you heard the story of the murder down by the Well House?"

Gannon felt a cold shiver slip down his spine. He narrowed his eyes at Bryan and said, "No."

Bryan's smile grew larger. "You should have Rich tell you. But, about hundred years ago, when all of this was farm land, two farmhands got into a fight for some reason. One of them was killed. It's an interesting story."

"I hadn't heard. That is interesting," said Gannon.

"Oh, there is a bunch of interesting stuff down there. One year we were fixing the pond and had to drain the water. We found an old faded red bicycle and a sledgehammer," continued Bryan.

"A red bike?" asked Gannon.

Bryan nodded and chuckled. "We probably would have found a dead body in there if we kept looking."

Gannon smiled. "Wouldn't surprise me."

# Part VI
# IN THE PAST

"NOOOO! Get off of me!" screamed Lucy as loud as she could.

Harvey clamped his hand over her mouth and hissed in her face, "Shut up!"

Lucy struggled under Harvey's strong grip. She didn't understand what was happening. She had agreed to go for a walk with Harvey by the pond. She had insisted that she bring her new bicycle. He seemed annoyed with her for insisting on bringing the bicycle. She tried to make him laugh by telling him silly jokes, but he would just smirk. Even though he seemed annoyed with her, he also appeared nervous. He kept looking over his shoulder and peering through the trees. Lucy knew they were alone because the sun had barely risen over the mountain top. She had gotten up early to do her chores, so she could ride her bike down to the road and back again before Pa started working in the fields. It surprised her that Harvey was already in the barn working. She had greeted him and then went about her chores. She felt him watching her, and for some reason that feeling made her uncomfortable today. When she caught Harvey looking at her, he would simply smile and nod his head. When she finished her chores and grabbed her bicycle, that was when he dropped down out of the loft like a bobcat and asked if she wanted to go for a walk to the pond. She didn't really want to go. She wanted to ride her bicycle. But he insisted. In return, she insisted on bringing her bicycle.

When they reached the pond, they walked around it once and stopped by the Well House. She thanked him for the walk and told him she was going to ride up to the road and back to the house. But he became angry with her, and she didn't understand why. He grabbed the bicycle from her and kept repeating "You owe me!" She kept thanking him for the bike, but he kept hissing, "I want more than your thanks!" She backed away from him in the hopes of finding a chance to jump on her bicycle and ride home. She believed if she could just get on her bicycle, she would be able to peddle fast enough to ride home to her Pa. When she backed far enough away from Harvey, she turned her bicycle and jumped on the seat. Before she could start to peddle, though, he lunged at her and grabbed the back wheel of the bicycle. He yanked on the wheel so hard that she was flung forward into the handlebars. Her crotch struck the middle bar and the air escaped her lungs from the immense pain that shot into her stomach. Harvey violently pushed her the rest of the way off the bicycle. Then she watched as he picked up the bicycle and threw it into the pond.

The bicycle made a loud splash and disappeared under the water. Tears streamed down Lucy's face with a mixture of pain and sadness. Harvey advanced on her and picked her up from the shoulders, squeezing her tight in a hug against his body. He kept whispering, "I'm sorry. I'm so sorry." Next thing she knew, he was pressing her against the rough stone wall of the Well House. He was rubbing her private areas through her work pants saying, "I'm sorry I hurt you." That's when she started to scream. He became angry. He wrapped both hands around her neck and started to choke her, hissing over and over again, "Shut up!" through clenched teeth.

Lucy fought as hard as she could. She kicked her legs, swung her arms, and tried to scream as loud as she could. Tears streamed down her eyes as she felt her lungs burn. In her mind, she kept screaming, but she didn't think any sounds were coming out of her mouth anymore. Harvey's hands were so big. So strong. So disgusting. She tried blinking away the blackness that crept into her eyes. She saw Joe-Michael standing behind Harvey with a sledgehammer before her world went black.

Joe-Michael swung the sledgehammer and struck Harvey in the knee. The young man released his grip on Lucy as he crumpled to the ground. Joe-Michael looked at the shocked expression on Harvey's face before swinging the sledgehammer a second time and crushing the young man's skull. Calmly, he dropped the sledgehammer at his feet. Picking up the young man's body, he tossed it into the pond as if it was a bale of hay. He then threw the sledgehammer into the water, turned back around, picked up Lucy in his arms and carried her home.

Joe-Michael met Lucy's father on the trail back to her house. Her father had heard Lucy's screams and started running toward her to help as well. Her father ran up to Joe-Michael and brushed the blonde hair from her face. He saw the finger length bruises already forming on her neck and asked, "What happened!?"

"Harvey, sir," stated Joe-Michael.

Joe-Michael watched as anger surged through Lucy's father's face and body. The man hissed through his teeth, "I'll kill that sonofabitch," and tried to step past Joe-Michael.

Joe-Michael side-stepped in front of Lucy's father and said, "That won't be necessary, sir."

Lucy's father stopped short and looked into Joe-Michael's eyes. He understood. Joe-Michael placed Lucy into his arms and turned to walk away.

Lucy's father called out, "Joe-Michael?"

Joe-Michael stopped and turned back toward the older man.

Lucy's father hesitated and then said, "I'm in need of a farmhand."

"I'd appreciate that. Thank you, sir," replied Joe-Michael.

Lucy's father gave Joe-Michael a nod. "No, thank you, Joe-Michael."

Joe-Michael gave a nod of appreciation.

"Let's get Lucy up to the house so her mother can care for her. Then we'll go talk to your boss," said Lucy's father.

Joe-Michael nodded in agreement and followed the older man up to the farmhouse.

# Part VII

# PRESENT

"What do you mean she died?" asked Gannon.

Rich shrugged. "Harvey had crushed her windpipe. There wasn't anything they could do. She slowly suffocated and died."

"What happened to Joe-Michael?" asked Farah.

"Not sure. Shortly after Lucy died, the family sold the farm and left. Rumor has it that Joe-Michael lived in the woods on Short Hill by the ole' mill for a number of years before disappearing," said Rich.

"Gah, what a horrible story," said Gannon.

Rich nodded in agreement. "We assume the past was more innocent than our own times, but that's not always the case."

Gannon nodded. Rich bid his farewell and descended the steps of the old Griffith house. Farah and Gannon watched Rich cross the stream and walk pass the old barn in the fading sunlight. As the man walked up the hill and disappeared through the row of trees, a blonde-haired girl of about ten years old stepped out of the trees onto the path. She glanced toward Gannon and Farah and waved. Farah gripped Gannon's hand tightly. A wave of relief washed over them as they stared at the girl. The little girl did a cartwheel down the hill and waved again. She then disappeared back into the trees. Gannon and Farah heard a soft, "Taa daaa" over the gentle breeze that rustled the branches of the trees.

## Thank you for reading!

What did you think of *The Well House*?

I would be grateful if you could leave a rating or review for this book at your favorite review site

(i.e., Goodreads, Amazon).

Reviews are a great way for indie authors to gain readers.

Thank you for your support!

## Follow My Work...

Twitter: @ErnestSolar
Instagram: @Ernestsolar
Facebook.com/spiritofsasquatch

SPIRIT OF
SASQUATCH

BY
ERNEST SOLAR

# ABOUT THE AUTHOR

**ERNEST SOLAR** has been a writer, storyteller, and explorer of one kind or another for his entire life. He grew up devouring comic books, novels, any other type of book along with movies, which allowed him to explore a multitude of universes packed with mystery and adventure. A professor at Mount St. Mary's University in Maryland, he lives with his family in Lovettsville, Virginia.

www.ingramcontent.com/pod-product-compliance
Lightning Source LLC
Chambersburg PA
CBHW020607130626
46552CB00007B/3086